Last Chance Quarterback

ALDEN ALL STARS

Last Chance Quarterback

Tommy Hallowell

PUFFIN BOOKS

PUFFIN BOOKS
Published by the Penguin Group
Viking Penguin, a division of Penguin Books USA Inc.,
375 Hudson Street, New York, New York 10014, U.S.A.
Penguin Books Ltd, 27 Wrights Lane, London W8 5TZ, England
Penguin Books Australia Ltd, Ringwood, Victoria, Australia
Penguin Books Canada Ltd, 2801 John Street, Markham, Ontario, Canada L3R 1B4
Penguin Books (N.Z.) Ltd, 182–190 Wairau Road, Auckland 10, New Zealand

Penguin Books Ltd, Registered Offices: Harmondsworth, Middlesex, England

First published in Puffin Books, 1990
1   3   5   7   9   10   8   6   4   2
Copyright © Daniel Weiss and Associates, 1990
All rights reserved

LIBRARY OF CONGRESS CATALOGING IN PUBLICATION DATA
Hallowell, Tommy.   Last chance quarterback / Tommy Hallowell.
p.   cm.–(Alden All Stars)
Summary: Sam tries to build his football team's confidence in his
abilities as quarterback and finally gets a chance to prove himself
at the end of the season.
ISBN 0-14-032909-9
[1. Football–Fiction.]   I. Title.   II. Series: Hallowell, Tommy.
Alden All Stars.
PZ7.H164Las   1990   [Fic]–dc20   89-78150

Printed in the United States of America
Set in Century Schoolbook

To Willie Stewart, who was there.

Last Chance Quarterback

1

Sam gripped the laces on the ball, planted his feet in the muddy field, cocked his arm, and let fly. The pass was perfect—just a little *too* long, in fact—forcing Nick to dive. Barely catching the ball, he did a full lay-out into a puddle with a terrific sliding splash.

Dennis Clements climbed off his bicycle on the nearby blacktop, hooting with delight. He had arrived just in time to see the Mud Bowl's first great play: Sam McCaskill to Nick Wilkerson for a major-league mess. Nick climbed slowly out of the mud. He threw the ball back to Sam, then took off his glasses to wipe them clean.

The three friends tossed the ball around, waiting for the other players to arrive. The Mud Bowl was a neighborhood tradition that had started one year when it rained on one of their backyard football games. The idea was partly to play football, but mostly to get completely covered in slimy mud. If the field wasn't muddy enough, they changed the rules and made everyone play on their knees, or played "Kill-the-guy-with-the-ball," or they practiced diving catches—directly over the largest puddle.

More players soon gathered on the field behind Fairwood, their old elementary school. As soon as the thunderclouds had rolled in over Cranbrook yesterday, Sam had gotten on the phone to recruit players. He was always the organizer. In addition to Nick and Dennis, Justin Johnson had agreed to come, along with Pete, Kyle, Dave, and Mark.

A drizzle was still coming down, but the late August morning was warm and the sun was beginning to peer through the clouds. Perfect Mud

Bowl weather. Sam was impatient for the game to start. As soon as the last player arrived, he took charge.

"Okay, listen up," Sam said. "Five-banana count, one blitz per series and one running play per series, three completes are a first. All right?"

The boys all nodded in agreement. They all knew the rules. They were used to playing a passing, tackle game, where instead of yard markers, a certain number of complete passes earned a first down.

"Dennis and I will pick teams," Sam continued.

"I get first pick, then," Dennis said. He wanted to keep Sam, the best quarterback in the bunch, from choosing Nick, the gang's best receiver. There was no way he would let Sam and Nick team up.

With the teams even at four players apiece, the Mud Bowl officially began. Dennis kicked the ball off a plastic tee. It went low and skipped off a puddle to the goal line, where Sam picked it up. As he started to run, Sam slipped and fell to one knee. He got up again and stomped up the wet field, moving so slowly he looked as if he was wearing snow boots. Dennis's team quickly caught up with him. They had him stopped, but Sam refused to go down. All eight players gathered, pushing and pulling before they collapsed into one giant pileup. From the bottom of the pile, Sam yelled, "I'm down, I'm down! Get off!"

The players untangled themselves. As they stood, they yelled with delight. Everyone was smeared with mud.

"Hiya, buddy!" Nick said, mashing a handful of mud on Justin's shirt. Everyone laughed. Nick was always clowning around. Justin pretended he wasn't going to do anything about it, but as Nick turned away, he rubbed his dirty sneaker on Nick's leg and ran off. Nick picked up a piece of mud and threw it at him.

"Hey! Quit it, you guys. Let's play," Sam said.

"Okay, okay," Nick said, holding his hands up.

They returned to the game. On the first play, Dennis's team used their blitz. Without counting five-banana, they charged across the line. Sam was swarmed but managed to lob the ball to Kyle, who caught it only to be tackled without gaining any yardage.

On the next play, Sam called for Pete to go long. Taking the hike, Sam kept his eyes on Mark, hoping to mislead the defense. As Mark made his cut to the sideline, Sam faked the throw. The rusher had counted five by now and was charging. Sam looked downfield and saw Pete break open. He threw immediately. Justin realized his mistake and desperately tried to catch up, but it was too late. Pete was beyond his reach. Sam's pass hit Pete chest-high. He managed to hold on to the wet ball and slog all the way to the end zone for a touchdown.

After the quick first score, each team took its turns trying to throw the slippery ball, but it was becoming awfully hard to handle. Soon Sam couldn't find any more clean spots on his clothes to wipe his hands and Nick was having the same problem with his glasses. No one could complete three passes for a first down, so every drive stalled. Justin, who was always thinking of new ideas, suggested that they change the rule and make it *two* completes for a first down. With the new rule it was easier to get a drive going and the game was more fun.

Sam took turns at quarterback with the other guys on his team. He knew everyone liked to have a chance to throw the ball. After two hours of football, no one was quite sure of the score. Sam figured his team was definitely ahead, by two or three touchdowns, but no one really cared. They were all exhausted from trudging in the muck. Thoughts turned to food, and lunchtime brought the Mud Bowl to an end.

Everyone cleared out except Sam, Dennis, Nick, and Justin. The four were the best of friends. They had been together since fourth grade and were known as the Four Musketeers, because when you saw one, the others weren't far behind. Sam was their unofficial leader. He was a take-charge guy. On the other hand, Dennis was the glue that kept them together because he was so easy to get along with. Nick was the spark plug, always quick with a joke. Justin, the smallest, was also the smartest, and a master of sports trivia. Somehow, the four were a perfect balance.

Now the four friends were two weeks away from entering the seventh grade of Alden Junior High School. They were looking forward to it because seventh grade meant much more than just a new school—seventh grade was the first year of organized football.

"Your brothers played football, right?" Sam asked Nick.

"Yeah, they did. Mike quit after tenth grade, but Bill played all the way through. He started on the varsity."

"Who's the coach at Alden?" Dennis asked.

"I think a new guy is going to coach the seventh-grade team. Mr. Bernheim coaches the eighth-graders."

"Did you guys get cleats yet?" Dennis wanted to know. They shook their heads. "I'm not sure which are the best kind. And what else do we need? They give us pads and uniforms, right?"

"I'm just gonna use my soccer cleats," Justin said.

"No way," Sam said. "You have to get football cleats, they're totally different."

"Yeah?"

"They've got thicker protection all around."

"And you have to get two practice jerseys," Dennis reminded them. "What positions are you guys going for?"

"You know me," Sam said. "Definitely quarterback."

"And I want to be a wide receiver," Nick announced.

"I was thinking about linebacker," Dennis said.

"That's a good idea," Sam said. "How about you, Justin?"

Justin weighed in at 86 pounds and Sam wasn't

sure about his friend's chances of making the team. Maybe Justin would have a chance at defensive back or receiver. He was, after all, quick on his feet.

"I don't know," Justin said, shaking his head. "Actually I may not go out for the team. I don't think I'm good enough."

"You've got to, man," Dennis said. "We stick together no matter what."

"You're good enough," Sam chipped in. "What about those interceptions today? You don't have to be so big to play cornerback or safety."

"Okay, guys, you've convinced me. I can see you won't be able to play without me." Justin smiled.

"You won't regret it," Sam said. "Think about it. Not only are we going to have full uniforms, but we're going to play with down markers, and referees."

"And goalposts and penalty flags," Dennis added, smiling.

"We're going to be great, a great team," Sam said.

"How can we lose?" Nick chimed in. "With the four of us running razzle-dazzle plays, banging heads, and tearing our opponents limb from limb?"

"Yeah!" the four growled loudly.

The first meeting of the team was next week, before the start of school. As the four friends continued to talk, the morning's cloud cover was blowing over. The mud in their hair and clothes was beginning to dry up, and they were getting hungry, so the Musketeers split up and went home. On his way, Sam tried to figure out how he could get past his mom without her throwing a fit.

2

Sam was putting the foam pads into his uniform pants when Justin came around from the next row of lockers half-dressed.

"So far, so good," Justin said, "but one of you guys has to help me lace up the shoulder pads."

Sam looked up. Justin turned his back to him and Sam could see where the two plastic plates met across the middle, laced up, but untied. Something didn't look quite right.

"Do those feel comfortable?" Dennis asked. He was standing next to Sam. Justin shrugged.

"Turn around," Sam said. Justin turned slowly, showing them the pads.

Sam knew a lot about football plays, strategies, teams, and pro players from all the football books that lined his shelves. But none of them said anything about how to get into your pads. Sam hated not knowing what to do.

Sam and Dennis looked at each other. They knew something was wrong. Were the pads too small? Maybe they were laced too tightly?

At that moment Coach Kramden walked by. The boys had met their coach yesterday at the introductory workout. Today was the first full-contact practice.

"You've got your shoulder pads on backward, son," Coach Kramden said, hardly looking up as he walked by. Justin blushed deep red with embarrassment. Sam and Dennis laughed. Sam was just glad it wasn't him.

Once dressed—properly, he hoped—Sam started for the locker-room door, but paused to look in the mirror. Though he was as big or bigger than most twelve-year-olds, he wasn't exactly Hulk Hogan. He shrugged up his shoulders to look mean, but even with the shoulder pads he just didn't look tough, not with a mouthful of braces and dark curly hair that stuck out all over.

Sam joined his friends as they jogged out to the field. Nick was wearing his helmet backward to tease Justin.

"Which way did they go? Which way did they go?" Nick asked.

"Oh, knock it off," Justin replied.

Nick playfully hit himself on the helmet. "Ow, it won't knock off!"

"Ha, ha, so funny I forgot to laugh," Justin said. "Here, I'll help you knock it off," he added, and hit the side of Nick's helmet.

"You're dead!" Nick yelled, pulling off his helmet and tackling Justin. They wrestled briefly, then got to their feet.

At the start of practice, Coach Kramden ran the players through calisthenics: jumping jacks, four-point squat thrusts, and a lot of stretches. Sam felt strange in his uniform. Moving around in all those pads took some getting used to. The shoulder pads especially seemed stiff and Sam wondered how easy it would be to throw a ball in them.

After warm-ups, Coach did some basic instruction on proper blocking and tackling methods. Yesterday, he had covered all the league rules on holding, pass interference, and other basic groundwork. He had also spoken at length about conditioning and his expectations for all members of the Alden Panthers. Coach seemed tough, but he didn't seem like the type to really blow up. He was a no-nonsense guy.

Things seemed pretty slow to Sam. There was a lot of groundwork to cover, and every time they learned something, Coach took the time to make sure all thirty players knew what they were doing. Plus, Sam already knew most of it. He was anxious to hear about quarterbacking: What alignments would the offense have? Would they pass much? Would the quarterback call his own plays? Sam wanted to be the quarterback, and nothing else. It was *the* position, the glory position.

Finally, as the shadows on the field started to grow long, Coach called the players together. Sam was surprised at how tired he was. It didn't seem like they had done that much, but his arms and legs ached.

"All right, boys, good work today," Coach began. "Don't forget that if you have time to run and lift weights outside practice you'll improve that much faster. Everyone can hit the showers now, but I want to see all those who are interested in playing in the backfield or as a receiver—quarterbacks, running backs, wide receivers—for just a few minutes before you go."

Only five players left the field.

"Oh, no," Sam whispered to Justin. "Everyone wants to handle the ball!"

Then another ten players began moving away, but half the team remained. Justin and Nick raised their hands when Coach asked who wanted to play receiver. Then Sam groaned to himself when five hands went up for quarterback. Even though he was sure he was the best, Sam didn't want to fight four guys for the spot.

"A lot of arms," Coach said. "I guess we'll have to see if the league will change the rules and allow five balls in the game at once."

No one responded.

"That was a joke, guys."

The players laughed nervously. They were all anxious about winning a starting position.

"Obviously you can't all play quarterback, but you'll all get a fair shot," Coach said, and then he sent them all in.

Sam eyed his competition. He recognized one of them from Fairwood, Jack Sylvester. Jack was a pretty good athlete, but Sam had seen him throw, and wasn't worried. Of the other three, one seemed too small to make it in such a key position. Sam smiled. What was he worried about? Once Coach saw *him* play, those guys might as well take up tiddly-winks.

On their way out of the locker room, each player was handed a playbook containing about forty pages of plays, signals, and training information. While most of the guys gave it a quick flip-through and stuffed it into their backpacks, Sam held it as though it were a bible. Standing outside the school waiting for Nick, with whom he shared rides home, he carefully turned over each page.

Sam had seen play diagrams many times before in his books. The circles were the standard symbol for defensive positions and the triangles stood for the offensive positions. But now the symbols and plays came alive for him: 24 Off-Tackle, End-Around, Quarterback Option. In each, Sam imagined himself at the center of the triangles, taking the snap and moving in the precise lines of the play as the helpless circles were pushed aside.

"Hey, you don't have to read the whole thing now," Nick said, as he came up behind Sam.

"I was just looking at it."

"Well, let's get going. My mom's waiting to drive us home."

They gathered up their stuff and headed out to the parking lot.

"This is the greatest thing ever," Sam said. "The greatest thing that has ever happened to us, Nick. We're playing on a real team, together. The Mc-Caskill-to-Wilkerson bomb connection will become a legend!"

"Easy for you to say," Nick said. "You've been playing quarterback since the second grade. Nobody can throw like you do. But there are a half-dozen guys going out for split end."

"Hey, you're not worried about making the team, are you?"

"Nah. With thirty players, they can't afford to cut anyone, but I might not be a starter—not at the position I want."

"Quit worrying," Sam said as they arrived at Mrs. Wilkerson's car. "Once I'm quarterback, you'll be my number-one receiver."

"Mr. Confident," Nick said with a smile.

"It's the only way to be."

3

Coach Kramden stood by the offensive huddle.

"Run a 28-Blue on two," he instructed. The team moved into formation. Sam took his place behind the center, wiping his hands nervously on his pants. He checked his teammates' positions. They only had one basic setup, an I-formation with the halfback lined up behind the fullback with two split ends. This play was a quarterback option to the left. As the team came set, Sam barked the call as fiercely as he could. The first numbers the quarterback called were just decoys, to keep the defense off balance, then the offense counted the number of "huts" so they could all start at the same time.

"Ninety-two! Ninety-two! Hut, hut!"

The center snapped the ball into Sam's hands. Suddenly he was at the center of a swirl of noise and motion. He pulled off the line left and watched the linebackers already in pursuit. One glance backward confirmed that his halfback was trailing him, ready for the lateral. Another glance told him that the cornerback had shucked off Justin's block and was cutting off the outside. Now the defensive end was closing in.

Sam stopped suddenly, jamming his back foot into the turf. The defensive end slapped at him with his arms, but his momentum carried him past Sam, who looked back across the field in the same instant his hand felt for the laces of the ball. Nick was speeding down the right side, all alone. Sam quickly lofted the ball back across the field as his pursuers and blockers all collapsed on top of him. The throw didn't have much on it, but it had enough. Nick slowed down, caught the lob easily, and raced downfield. Sam climbed on his feet in time to see Nick stop running and hold the ball aloft. Sam clenched a fist in happiness.

"28-Blue is a running play," Coach Kramden said sternly.

Sam's smile disappeared fast.

"What's the 28-Blue, quarterback?"

"Quarterback option," Sam said, almost choking on the words.

"And what are the options?"

"To run it myself or lateral to the halfback."

"That's right. Okay, huddle up."

Sam was confused. His throat tightened. Only sheer willpower kept his eyes from tearing up. *I knew that,* he thought to himself. *I knew the options. I know every play by heart. I just saw that the run was dead. Why should I get criticized for throwing the first complete pass of the day?* Angry and embarrassed, Sam didn't dare say anything to Coach. He didn't want to make things worse. He just wouldn't make the same mistake ever again. From now on he would do *exactly* as Coach instructed.

In the huddle, Dennis distracted Sam with an elbow to the ribs.

"Hey, nice pass, anyhow," he said quietly.

"Oh, yeah?" Sam said. Then he shook his head. "That doesn't matter."

"All right," Coach interrupted. "64-Blue. Post. On three."

Sam concentrated tensely, but his spirits lifted at the call. It was a passing play, with the primary receiver, the left end, running a post pattern. *Maybe Coach did notice my throw,* Sam thought. *Maybe he wants to see if I can throw another one.*

Sam ran the play through in his mind as he stepped to the line. He could imagine the receiver running down the sideline, then breaking toward the goalpost. He was ready. Sam took the snap, back-pedaled, stepped on his fullback's foot—and fell down. Before he could even think of getting back up, he was buried. Sam gritted his teeth. It seemed like he couldn't buy a break.

"No huddle, same play," Coach said as the players got up. "Get on the line. And fire off, you guards. Get a jump on the defense."

On the third hut, Sam took the ball and back-pedaled without a problem. The end broke open. Sam set and fired. The pass was a perfect spiral, a real bullet. But it flew ten feet over the receiver and landed fifteen yards beyond his reach.

Sam watched in disbelief. He clasped his hands together on top of his helmet. *Great work, McCaskill. Very impressive.*

The next three plays were simple handoffs. The fullback dropped one, which wasn't Sam's fault, but he still figured it made him look bad. Coach looked down at his clipboard.

"Okay, let's have Barry Sanderson in at quarterback. Bob Donovan, halfback. Larry Stiles, fullback."

Coach also called out new names for the defense, but Sam wasn't listening. He stood on the sideline feeling lousy. Real football was turning out to be a lot different from backyard games. When he didn't get to play at quarterback, practice was boring, and when he did get in, everything seemed to go wrong. Sam never relaxed. When he was left standing around he ran through plays in his head and tried to remember everything Coach had instructed him. Sam had already memorized the entire playbook: twenty offensive plays, mostly basic runs, along with five defensive alignments, one formation each for kickoffs, receiving kickoffs, receiving punts, punting, and a fake punt (about the trickiest play in the whole book). None of the great school-yard plays were there; there was an end-around, but no double reverse, no Statue of Liberty, no halfback pass. It was straight-ahead, knock-'em-down, three-yards-and-a-cloud-of-dust football.

Sam understood Coach's reasons for keeping their offense simple, though. In practice the team was having trouble executing the most basic plays. Everyone had a lot to learn.

But being a little bored wasn't Sam's biggest worry. Lately, a disturbing thought had crossed his mind: What if Coach *didn't* name him the starting quarterback? Sam tried to put the idea out of his mind. He knew he was the best man for the position. He just hadn't had the chance to show it yet. Two of the original five contenders had dropped out. That left Sam, Barry Sanderson, and Jack Sylvester. Barry was quick on his feet and, despite his small size, was having some success running the ball. Jack was also a decent runner, but his few passes had shown little skill.

Before practice was over that day, Sam got in for another half-dozen plays. He handed the ball off four times, ran a QB sneak for three yards, and threw an incomplete pass. He was more frustrated than ever. And because Coach made everyone learn both an offensive and defensive position, Sam also played at cornerback. He didn't pay much attention to his defense, though. He wanted only to play quarterback. He was sure that once he earned the starting QB slot Coach would use him exclusively on the offense.

After practice, Sam, Justin, Nick, and Dennis walked back to the locker room together.

"On a scale of one to ten," Justin began.

"Zero," Nick interrupted.

"You haven't even heard the question," Justin said with a laugh.

"Was it something like, 'How much did I enjoy today's practice?' "

"As a matter of fact it was."

"I sure hope games are more fun," Dennis said.

"Yeah, it's really hard work," Justin agreed.

"What the matter with you, Sam?" Dennis asked. "You're not saying anything."

"Maybe he *likes* practice," Nick cracked.

"No, not exactly," Sam said quietly. "I was just thinking."

"Well, I think I'm the worst player on the team," Justin said seriously.

"No way!" Dennis said.

"Name somebody worse."

"Well, a lot of guys. Carl Mulligan is totally uncoordinated," Dennis said.

"Yeah, but he's *big*."

"You're as good as Jimmy Carlisle," Nick said.

Justin laughed. "I wish."

"Hey, Nick," Sam said, "let's hurry and shower quickly, okay? I can see my mom's car and I really want to get home soon."

"Yeah, all right," Nick said. "But what's the big hurry?"

"Gotta study for a math test."

Sam could tell his friends thought he was acting a little weird. He couldn't help it. There was so much to think about. Playing for the Alden Panthers wasn't the only thing new about seventh grade. His schoolbooks were heavier than ever—the biology book alone was two inches thick!—and in just the first week Sam had discovered the true meaning of homework. Since he didn't get home from practice until six-thirty, studying seemed to fill his whole evening. And he had to get to bed at a decent hour so he could get up early enough for his morning run. He was beginning to understand why his parents slept so late on weekends.

Sam stuffed his dirty uniform into a bag and grabbed his books. He walked out of the locker room. Coach Kramden was checking his clipboard against the bulletin board. Sam thought about saying good night, but Coach seemed distracted, so he just walked by. As he passed, Coach glanced up at him.

"Shoe's untied, Steve."

Sam looked behind him. Then he looked down at his sneaker, which had come undone. *Steve! Coach still doesn't know my name,* he thought. He set down

24

his bag and books and bent down to tie his laces. Sam wanted to correct the mistake, but he was too embarrassed to say anything. When he stood up, Coach gave him a quick nod and smile. *Say something,* Sam thought, but he didn't.

4

Sam called the play. "64-Red."

"Twenty-two! Nineteen! Hut!"

He stepped back quickly, surveying the field.

He zeroed in on the open man and threw the ball. The pass was on the mark, a low, hard spiral. Then all at once Sam saw trouble. It wasn't a safety in on the interception; it was the ditch.

"Watch out for the ditch, Charlie!" Sam yelled.

But it was too late. Charlie, Sam's eight-year-old brother, was too intent on catching the pass to pay

attention to the ditch between their yard and the
street. He jumped up and got both hands on the ball
at the same moment he ran off the lawn and into
two feet of mucky water. He toppled in with a terrific
splash.

Sam rushed across the yard. When he arrived
Charlie was just getting up, completely soaked, with
bits of wet leaves and debris all over him.

"I caught it!" Charlie said triumphantly, holding
up the ball with both hands. Sam had to laugh.

"Nice catch, superstar," he said. "And did you
catch any pollywogs while you were in there?"

Charlie flipped the ball to Sam and waded out of
the ditch. He looked himself over.

"Now you're eligible for our next Mud Bowl," Sam
declared.

"Is Mom gonna kill me?"

"Why don't you go in and lie down on the good
couch and find out?"

"Ha, ha."

Sam hosed his brother clean and they continued
with football practice. Charlie flipped through Sam's
playbook and picked different plays. On runs, Charlie was a running back, and on passing plays, he was
the receiver. Even though Charlie was little, he
could already catch the ball—sometimes even when

27

Sam threw it hard. He loved playing football with his older brother, even when it meant missing Saturday morning cartoons. He was proud to help Sam prepare for the Alden team.

Their sister Jill came out to join them. She was ten and almost as fast a runner as Sam. With the three of them playing, Sam soon gave up on practicing the plays. Instead, they played interception, with Charlie and Jill taking turns going out for a pass and covering on defense. By the time Mrs. McCaskill called them in for lunch they were all tired, and Charlie's clothes were dry again.

While munching sandwiches, they talked about their first week in new grades. Charlie's third-grade teacher was someone new, but Jill had Mrs. Gustaffson, who had been one of Sam's favorite teachers.

"So what's different at Alden?" Jill asked.

"Well," Sam said, "you change classes more because there are six periods a day. Otherwise, it's not really different or harder, except for the homework."

"When is the first football game?" Charlie asked.

"Not for another week. Next Friday afternoon."

"You're the quarterback, right?" Jill asked.

"Sam's always the quarterback," Charlie said. He looked to Sam for confirmation.

"Actually, I'm not officially anything yet."

"See," Jill said to her younger brother triumphantly.

"But you *will* be the quarterback," Charlie said.

"I better be. Coach Kramden will probably name the starters early next week. I haven't done very well yet, but I will."

The conversation got Sam worrying again. He had to do better and *soon*. Playing quarterback was all he had ever wanted to do. He knew he was good. He knew he was better than Barry or Jack, so why couldn't he prove it in practice?

After lunch, Dennis phoned. He was getting up a football game at the school yard.

Sam dashed downstairs, grabbed his ball, and headed out. Then he turned and went back inside the house.

"Mom! I'm going to play football. I'll be back for dinner!" he yelled from just inside the door.

"Again?" his dad asked as he came in from the garage where he did his woodworking. "You've been playing football every afternoon this week. Don't you want a day off?"

"This is different," Sam explained. "Football practice is like, well, practice. This is just for fun."

"Don't you have any fun at team practice?"

"Yeah, sure I do, but it's not the same. I don't

know," he shrugged. Sam opened the door to go.

"All right. Have a good time. Here," his dad said, putting out his hands, "let me have one toss."

Sam flipped him the ball as they stepped outside.

"Gimme the bullet, Dad!" he yelled as he ran a pattern toward the end of the driveway.

"You sure you want it?"

"Yeah, c'mon."

His dad threw. The ball zinged in a beeline. Sam put out his hands and caught the ball. It stung his palms.

"Not bad!" his dad said. "Maybe you should be playing receiver."

"No, thanks," Sam said, shaking out his hands.

"Have a good time."

"I will."

Sam climbed on his bike and pushed off. When he reached the street, Charlie came running out the front door.

"Hey! Can I play?"

"Big guys' game, sorry!" Sam yelled over his shoulder. He pedaled quickly toward Fairwood.

Nick, Justin, Dennis, Kyle, and Pete were discussing the rules when Sam climbed off his bike to join them.

"Hey, Sam, what do you say to playing two-hand

touch?" Justin asked. "I'm feeling kind of sore from practice."

"Yeah," Nick agreed. "How come we finally get to wear pads and end up getting twice as bruised?"

"I know what you mean," Sam said. "Two-hand touch is fine with me. Let's choose up sides."

After the kickoff, Sam huddled with his team.

"I'll start at quarterback, okay?" he asked, and then called the play. "Justin, you run a deep Z-pattern. Kyle, you stay short in case Justin's not open."

The Z-pattern was just what it sounded like. Justin cut across, zigged back and deep downfield, then zagged back again. Nick was with him the whole way, but as Justin made him last cut, Sam whipped the ball. The pass spun through the air like a drill. Nick leapt but Justin had a crucial half-step lead. His outstretched hands snared the ball and, as Nick rolled onto the ground, Justin jogged past the end line for a touchdown.

All afternoon, the football obeyed Sam's every command. The tension from practice and performing in front of Coach Kramden disappeared. Sam threw long and threw short with pinpoint accuracy. His team was far ahead by the time Justin checked the watch he had hanging on his bike. He had to go, so the game broke up.

Sam and Nick rode home together, tired and grass-stained.

"So how come you don't play like that in practice," Nick teased.

Sam frowned.

"Sore point, sorry."

"No, no problem. I just . . . I wish I knew. The harder I try, the more I mess up. Having Coach looking over my shoulder all the time, it's hard to concentrate."

"I know what you mean," Nick said. "Plus it's difficult getting used to all the plays, and the pads and everything. It's a lot different than I thought it would be."

"Yeah, but I'm still mad at myself. It shouldn't make a difference. What if I don't get to be starting quarterback?"

"Aww, you're better than Barry or Jack."

"Maybe, but does Coach know that? I sure haven't shown him much."

They were just arriving at Nick's house. Nick waved and turned off into his drive while Sam kept going.

Even though they had played touch, Sam was sore and tired. He had been throwing footballs all day long, and his arm was worn out. Still, he felt good.

In fact, he felt great. His old confidence was back. He believed Nick. He believed he was better than Barry and Jack. He remembered how it felt to run an offense, and knew that if he got the chance he could run the Alden offense. Sam felt like a quarterback again.

Now all he had to do was play as well in next week's practices.

5

On Monday morning a storm was brewing. All day the sky grew darker until, all at once, the rain came down. Sam and Justin were sitting together in biology class when the heavy drops started drumming against the windows. The whole class began to murmur, and a few students got up from their seats to get a better look.

"All right, everyone," Mr. Evans said, attempting to keep order. "I think we've all seen rain before."

The class calmed down enough for Mr. Evans to

continue his lecture on the parts of a cell. But Sam's thoughts were elsewhere, and so were Justin's. He slid a note to Sam: *Do we have to practice when it rains? Maybe we can practice in the gym?*

Sam wrote his answer on the same sheet: *Outdoor practice, rain or shine, hail or snow.*

Yeecchhh, Justin wrote.

They began to whisper.

"I really don't want to practice in this weather," Justin said.

"Just think of it as a Mud Bowl."

"Can you imagine doing those 'hit it' drills?" Justin said. They both winced at the thought of having to jog in place until Coach yelled "Hit it," and then throw themselves on the ground, chest-first, only to scramble back to their feet as quickly as possible. Coach would also yell: "Hit it, roll left," and "Hit it, roll right."

"I'm just going to hit it the first time," said Sam, "bury myself, and hope Coach doesn't see me."

Justin laughed too loudly.

"I don't think of cellular meiosis as especially funny, Justin," Mr. Evans said.

Justin gulped and tried to look serious. "No, sir."

"Maybe you can tell the class what meiosis is?"

Sam crossed his fingers that he wouldn't be called on next.

"Meiosis," Justin began, "is, uh, the division of the cell into reproductive cells with half the number of chromosomes."

"That's correct," a surprised Mr. Evans admitted. They were off the hook. The biology teacher turned back to his lecture.

Sam stared at Justin in disbelief. Justin half-smiled, a little embarrassed to have known the answer, and whispered: "I read ahead over the weekend, that's all."

Sam shook his head and decided he had better start paying attention. Maybe Justin didn't have to listen, but *he* sure did.

The rain was still falling as the team rolled out for practice that afternoon. As they walked out to the field, Nick, Dennis, and Sam were still trying to convince Justin that practicing in the mud might be fun.

"It'll be uncomfortable," Justin argued. "And a guy could catch a cold. Not to mention the mess."

"But you like playing in the Mud Bowls," Sam pointed out.

"That's different."

"How?"

"It's warmer, for one thing."

"It's not that cold."

"Look, just give me one logical reason why we can't practice inside when it rains. C'mon, Sam, you seem to know everything about football."

"Well, you can't do tackling drills, for one."

"Sure, you can't do tackling drills or live scrimmages on the gym floor, but there are other things to do," Justin said.

"Does there have to be a logical explanation for everything?" Nick asked.

"Yes, as a matter of fact," Justin answered.

"There's Coach Kramden," Sam said. "If you're so sure we should be practicing in the gym, why don't you go ask him why we can't."

"All right," Justin said. "I will."

Sam and Dennis watched in surprise as Justin marched across the field toward Coach Kramden, who was cloaked in a large gray poncho. They kept waiting for Justin to turn around and come back, but he didn't stop until he was face-to-face with the coach.

"Radical!" Dennis exclaimed. "He's actually doing it."

Sam shook his head. "He's going to make a fool of himself."

They watched as Justin and Coach Kramden talked. Justin was nodding. Finally, he turned and made his way back to the guys.

"Well, what did Coach say?" Dennis asked.

"He had a very logical reason. What if it rains in a game? We should practice under the same conditions we might have to play under."

They all had to admit that Coach was right. Sam wished he had thought of the explanation. He was still surprised at Justin's easy way of talking to Coach. He wished it were that easy for him, but it just wasn't. Sam had always found it difficult talking to adults. And since he felt that he still hadn't impressed Coach with his football ability, Sam was even more nervous about facing him one-on-one. He could answer Coach's questions during practice, but was too nervous to ask any of his own.

After the first few times the players "hit it," everyone was soaked. Sam was anxious to run plays so he could try to guess who Coach was favoring at quarterback. If Coach had Barry run the first series, did that mean Barry was the number-one quarterback? If Sam got to run two more passing plays than Jack, did that mean Coach thought he had a better arm? Jack had become the team's punter and kicker; did that give him an edge on QB? Who did Coach talk to most? Who got the most playing time? Sam didn't get any answers. Not today. Practice was just one blocking drill after another.

At one point, Sam faced off against Barry Sanderson in a blocking drill. His adrenaline shot up as he looked squarely at one of his competitors for the QB slot. He shot out of his stance and knocked his smaller opponent back off the line. For now, Barry and Jack were his enemies. Sam wouldn't give an inch. No smiles, no chat, no "may the best man win." His two competitors had been friendly at first, but were surprised at Sam's cutthroat attitude. Now they just steered clear.

6

When Sam went for his early run the next morning, his thoughts were focused on being quarterback. He knew his performance at practice had not been impressive, but what more could he do? He had learned the playbook backward, forward, and sideways. He had just about worn out Jill and Charlie with his home passing sessions. He was running in the mornings and lifting weights whenever he could. *Why can't I play my best in front of Coach?* he thought. *Am I a choke artist who can't take a little pressure?*

Sam was so distracted that he ran farther than usual. By the time he got home the school bus had come and gone. Luckily, his dad could drop him off on his way to work.

"Are you sure your coach told you to run on days you have practice?" Mr. McCaskill asked in the car. "It seems like an awful lot of exercise."

"Not really, Dad. We spend a lot of practice time just standing around listening."

"Is it fun?"

"Fun?"

"Well, fun, satisfying, whatever. Do you like it?"

"Of course I do," Sam answered. "I mean, things will be more interesting once we get into games and all."

"You're still tense about making quarterback, huh?"

Sam just nodded.

"I know you've looked forward to this for a long time, but don't put too much pressure on yourself, Sam. After all, this is your first year of organized football."

"But it's the first year for everyone on the seventh-grade team. That's no excuse."

"Well, I didn't mean it as an excuse. I just think you'll be happier—and probably play better—if you learn to relax a little, that's all."

Sam knew it was good advice. He had heard it before. But even though Sam realized that he drove himself pretty hard, the more he told himself to relax, the more wound up he got. He was convinced only one thing could cure him: if Coach named him starting quarterback.

His dad dropped him off and Sam scooted to his first-period class. Maybe a little math would take his mind off football.

It didn't. Neither did English, social studies, health, gym, or biology. Even the lunch hour seemed to last forever. The day dragged until Sam stuffed his books into his locker and headed for practice.

The field was still wet, but the sun was shining and it was warm. After the calisthenics and warm-ups, Coach set up scrimmage teams. Sam was glad they were running plays, so he didn't mind that Coach started him at cornerback.

The first play was an off-tackle run that Tim Lopatt broke for five yards. On the next play Jack lateraled the ball to Bob Donovan, who came around Sam's end. Justin, at split end, led the blocking, but

Sam sidestepped him. Bob then tried to get outside, but Sam put his head down and grabbed both the runner's legs, bringing him down easily. Dennis helped Sam to his feet and they slapped hands.

"Good tackle!" Coach said. "That's what I've been telling all you cornerbacks to do. You've got to protect the outside. Turn the play back into the middle."

Sam's spirits lifted. Coach Kramden had finally praised him for something. All those tackling drills had paid off.

When Coach rearranged the lineups, he left Sam at cornerback. Barry replaced Jack at quarterback and on his third play, ran the option and kept the ball for a long gain. Sam watched him in frustration. He couldn't help wishing that Barry would mess up. Jack, too. Whenever they did particularly well, it made him nervous.

A few plays later, Sam set up opposite Alan Broadstreet, who was at wide receiver. Alan's intense concentration and nervous movements told Sam that this was a passing play. *Interception,* he thought. *I'll pick off Barry's pass and take it all the way to the end zone.*

Barry took the hike and faded into the pocket just

as Sam had guessed. Alan took off, but Sam stayed with him step for step. It was a down-and-out pattern. Sam glanced upfield to see Barry rolling to his right. He hung back a little, trying to hide so Barry would try the pass. Barry put up the ball. Sam leapt high in the air. He snagged it. He landed on his feet and took off running. Coach blew his whistle and the players stopped chasing him.

Sam was eager for Coach to take note of his play. He was pleased to see Coach give him a nod, but then Coach turned his attention to the offensive linemen, showing them something about pass blocking.

Practice started to drag for Sam. It seemed like Barry remained at quarterback for a long time before Coach gathered the team together and rearranged their positions again.

"Quarterback, Sam McCaskill."

Sam was relieved to hear his name. He was getting another chance to prove himself. *Maybe going last is best,* he thought. *If I do well, Coach will remember it.* The players gathered with Sam in the offensive huddle. He wiped his hands nervously.

"All right, Sam, really push those handoffs into the runners' guts," Coach instructed. "Run a 24-Blue."

Sam pounded the ball into Tim, who busted up the middle for twelve yards before Justin, playing safety, managed to grab hold of him and slow him down until help arrived for the tackle.

The next few plays were handoffs, then Sam ran a quarterback option, keeping the ball but gaining only a yard. The next play was 58-Blue, a passing play with the primary receiver cutting across the middle.

Sam took the snap and faded back to the right side. The defensive rush was on him, but he saw his man open. He quickly lobbed the ball across the middle. It was on target, but the coverage was tight, forcing the receiver to drop the ball.

Sam wondered if he should have looked for another receiver, or even kept the ball and run. Suddenly his thoughts were interrupted and he realized that Coach had been saying something to him.

"Do you understand?" Coach asked. Sam wasn't sure. He thought Coach had said something about making the pass "straighter." Did he mean to throw the pass harder and lower?

"Yeah, I understand," Sam said, not wanting to seem stupid by asking Coach to repeat himself.

"Okay, try a 60-Blue."

"60-Blue. Got it."

Sam went into the huddle uncertainly. His last pass was pretty low and straight to start with. 60-Blue was a pass with the tight end as first-choice receiver. Sam called the play, broke huddle, and stepped up to the line.

"Forty-two! Sixteen! Hut!"

He stepped backward, moving to the right, following the receiver with his eyes. He was a step ahead of the linebacker. Making sure to throw the ball on a beeline, Sam let it loose. It was a bullet. The tight end got one hand on it, but there was no way he could catch it. Sam groaned to himself. Why couldn't anything go right?

Coach Kramden took off his glasses and rubbed the top of his nose.

"What did I say last play, Sam?"

"I don't know," Sam said nervously. "I mean, throw it straight. Right?"

"No, I said I wanted you to fade straight back in the pocket," Coach said patiently. "You're almost rolling out. Go straight back and you give the linemen a chance to protect you and it leaves you more options on your pass. Straight back."

As Coach spoke, Sam felt a wave of hopelessness come over him. Everything he did was wrong. Sam ran a few more plays but his confidence was shot. Instead of working to make the plays, he was just trying to avoid mistakes. He was second-guessing himself on every move. And that was no way to play quarterback.

7

On Wednesday, at the beginning of practice, Coach Kramden assembled the players on the bleachers. The moment of truth had come. Everyone knew that he was about to read the starting lineups for Friday's game against North Colby. The players all tried hard to look relaxed.

"I've chosen a starting lineup for offense and defense," Coach began. "Now if you don't hear your name, don't think your career is over, all right?

Everyone on this team will play football—at least one quarter every game. You've all worked hard and you all deserve to play. We're going to do our best to win—but *everyone* will participate."

Sam was so nervous he could barely listen. He carefully retied the laces on his cleats. Nick, Dennis, and Justin sat with him, and Sam could tell that they were worried, too. Finally, Coach flipped a few sheets on his clipboard and read the lineup. Sam's name was the very first one he read.

"Sam McCaskill, left cornerback."

Sam's heart leapt and fell. Cornerback.

Dennis, Justin, and Nick all looked at him, smiling. Even though they knew Sam wanted nothing but quarterback, they thought it was great to be a starter. Dennis put out his hand for a slap, but Sam shook his head. He had a bad feeling that the starting slot at cornerback meant somebody else would run the offense. Coach kept reading.

The positions filled quickly. Dennis was starting at linebacker. Nick was one of four split ends who would rotate in on every down, so that Coach could send in the plays from the sideline. Tim Lopatt was the fullback and Bob Donovan the halfback. Justin's name wasn't called.

"Starting quarterback will be Barry Sanderson."

Sam didn't react. He saw Dennis glance at him, but he tried hard not to let the disappointment show in his blank stare.

Coach finished reading his list and tucked his clipboard under his arm.

"Now, I know that some of you will be disappointed. Believe me when I say it was very difficult making these decisions. And these slots aren't carved in stone. I'm sure as the season progresses there will be changes."

Coach Kramden went on to explain how he would be changing positions around, shifting people in on offense and defense since everyone was still learning the game, but by now Sam had tuned out. He had been beaten out at quarterback. There was no way around that. He thought maybe he had done *too* well at cornerback. He had tried so hard to stop Barry and Jack's passes—and the effort had backfired on him. He also thought Coach hadn't given him enough time to prove himself. But Sam quickly realized he was just making excuses, and he felt even worse. *I tried, I messed up,* he thought. *Maybe I should just quit.*

When Coach ended the sit-down talk, the group

clambered down from the bleachers. Justin slapped Sam on the back.

"Congratulations," he said.

"For what?" Sam said flatly.

"Don't give me that," Justin said, almost angry. "At least you've got a starting position."

Sam was embarrassed.

"I'm sorry, Justin, I'm just . . . I know I should be happy, but I wanted to play quarterback."

"Yeah, yeah," Justin said impatiently.

"We're all going to get to play," Dennis said, but neither Sam nor Justin seemed to believe it.

As they reached the field, Sam jogged by Coach, who was talking to Jack Sylvester, but he slowed and turned around when he heard his name called. Coach waved him over. Jack had left.

"Sam, I know you're probably not happy about the quarterback situation. You gave a real good effort and did well. I just think Barry and Jack did better."

"Uh huh." Sam nodded. *Two guys?!* he thought. *I'm third-string?* But Coach wasn't done yet.

"Jack will be backing up Barry, so unless there is an injury or something I'm going to have you concentrate full-time on defense for now."

"Okay."

"Is that all right?"

"Sure, fine."

Sam just wanted to get away. He quickly turned and jogged off.

Sam directed his pent-up frustration into practice. He played furiously, pursuing every play until he was breathless. He could hardly stand still long enough to huddle and jiggled his legs nervously as the defensive play was called. He tossed aside blockers and tackled runners with ferocity. On the one pass that got by him and into Nick's hands, he brought down his friend with a tackle so hard it knocked the ball loose.

"Geez, take it easy," Nick said angrily.

"Can't stand the heat, get out of the kitchen," Sam replied.

"What're you talking about?"

Sam realized what he was saying, and to whom, and put out a hand to pull Nick up.

"I guess I'm just feeling a little bloodthirsty," Sam said. Nick understood. All of Sam's friends knew how much the quarterback slot had meant to him.

At the end of practice Sam walked by Coach.

"Played aggressively today, McCaskill. Good work."

Sam gave a half-nod, but didn't say anything. He didn't care what Coach Kramden thought anymore and, of course, he didn't tell him that during all those bone-rattling tackles he'd pretended it was Kramden he was taking down.

At home that evening Sam avoided talking with his family. He just closed the door to his room and tried to do homework until dinner. His parents left him alone. They seemed to guess what his mood meant, but Charlie couldn't figure it out.

"Did you throw a touchdown in practice today?" Charlie asked at the dinner table.

"Didn't play quarterback today."

"Why not?"

"Just didn't."

"Aren't you going to be quarterback at the game?"

"No."

"Why not?"

Mr. McCaskill interrupted his younger son. "I think that's enough about football, Charles."

The rest of dinner was pretty quiet. Sam had nothing to say, and he barely finished the first of his usual three helpings of food. He excused himself early and went to his bedroom, where he sat in front of the same page of his biology book for a long while. His dad knocked on his door later.

"Come in," Sam said. He liked his dad, but at times like this he just wanted to be alone. After all, what was there to say? He hadn't made quarterback and he didn't want any sympathy.

"I know you're disappointed," Mr. McCaskill began. "What did your coach say?"

"The usual 'you all worked hard,' et cetera, et cetera."

"I'm sure you'll get a chance to play."

"Yeah, well, actually I'm starting on defense," Sam said.

"That's super. Where?"

"Cornerback."

"Well, that's a great spot," his dad said, but Sam just shrugged. "Sam, you've got to learn to use this disappointment in a positive way. It may sound wrong-headed, but it could be good for you."

Sam nodded. He didn't feel any better, though. Pep talks were for losers.

Shortly after his dad left, Charlie came in. He sat on Sam's bed.

"If you really try hard you can still be the quarterback," he said.

"How do you figure?" Sam said.

"You just have to try again. The coach will see how good you are and then he'll make you the quarterback. You're the best thrower, the best runner, and the best . . . what else does the quarterback do?"

"Handoffs."

"You're the best at that, too."

Things were simpler for Charlie. Instead of arguing with him, Sam just put him off.

"I'll take your advice, okay?"

"Okay."

Sam turned back to his book. Charlie stayed on Sam's bed, flipping through a copy of *Sports Illustrated*.

"Did you want something else?" Sam asked.

"Can't I just sit here?"

"No. I'm trying to study."

"I'm just sitting here. . . ."

"Sit in your own room."

"C'mon, I'm not . . ."

"Do I have to call Dad?"

"All right, all right," Charlie said, angrily hopping off the bed. "I'm going."

He paused at the door for a moment, trying to think of the meanest thing he could say.

"I hope they use your head for a ball!" Charlie said. Sam had to laugh. His little brother wasn't very good at insults yet.

If only things were as simple as Charlie said, thought Sam. *Just try hard and you get what you want. But I already gave it my best shot. What more can I do?*

8

"It'll never happen. It's as simple as that. I'll never play quarterback again."

"C'mon, Sam," Dennis said, but Sam interrupted him.

"Don't give me any advice, Dennis. I don't need a pep talk or any of that cheese."

The two were walking to the gym to dress for their first game.

"But you heard Coach, things can change."

"Oh, sure, if I play cornerback really well maybe

he'll put me in at quarterback? That makes a lot of sense."

"Maybe you should tell him you want a second chance."

"Forget it, okay?"

"Okay, okay," Dennis said. "All I know is that I think you're still the best quarterback for this team."

That afternoon the Alden Panthers were scheduled to play North Colby. They didn't know much about them. As a matter of fact, they didn't know too much about any of their opponents. They would play five games: North Colby, Williamsport, South Colby, Lincoln, and Bradley.

Colby was the biggest city in the area and, like Cranbrook, had two junior high schools, North and South. Cranbrook had both Alden and Abraham Lincoln Junior High. Naturally, Lincoln was Alden's big rival. Williamsport and Bradley usually had the best athletic programs, but seventh-grade sports had all new players, so it was hard to predict which teams would come out on top.

Despite himself, Sam was pretty excited as he pulled on his game jersey. He had tried it on before, but this time was for real. He looked at the bright white number, twenty-two, against the dark green background. Not bad, not bad at all.

Though he still felt angry and disappointed about not making quarterback, Sam was ready to play. It had been a shock realizing that he could want something and not get it. Ever since the first grade he had been able to run faster, throw farther, and climb higher than his friends. He was used to being the best. Sam thought maybe it had been *too* easy for him. He tried to believe what his dad had said, that this might be good for him. But deep down, he believed what Charlie and Dennis had said more: that if he just got another chance, he *could* be the quarterback.

For the time being, he wasn't going to quit. He was going to play the best game of cornerback Coach Kramden had ever seen.

The game was at home, but shifted over to the eighth-grade field. There were goalposts and they had marked out the gridiron with the lime machine. The eighth-grade game would be played after theirs was over. The field was dry and the sun was shining.

The guys were talking loudly on the sideline. Mr. Boyd, one of the gym teachers, was acting as Coach Kramden's assistant. But even the two of them had trouble quieting everyone down. Coach never raised his voice, so it took a minute to realize he was getting angry. Finally everyone came more or less to order.

After some details, Coach had Barry and Dennis run the team through calisthenics. Sam still felt like Barry had stolen his job. Dennis was doing well at linebacker.

At the opening whistle, Sam tried to put all his worries aside. Jack kicked off, a low bouncing kick that North Colby returned to about the forty. As he took to the field with the Alden defense, Sam snapped on his helmet and popped in his mouth guard.

It was strange looking across the line at someone you had never seen before. The first play was a quick run into the line. The end push-blocked Sam. As soon as Sam saw the tackle, and heard the play whistled dead, he stood upright. At that moment the end threw one more block, knocking Sam back on his heels. Sam was mad.

"All right, junior," he said sarcastically to the skinny split end. "We're all pretty excited, but when the play's over it's over."

The second play was busted immediately after the quarterback mishandled the snap and fell on the ball for a two-yard loss. It was third and long, but Sam guessed that they would handle this first possession conservatively. He was right. It was a halfback run around his end.

The pursuit wasn't good. The Alden linemen had

been thinking pass and committed themselves inside. Sam was on his own. "Junior" was coming at him fast and low while the back was speeding up behind him.

Sam let the end come to him, then put both hands on top of his opponent's helmet and pushed straight down. The end hit the dirt and Sam skipped over him to grab the surprised halfback for a loss.

Back-slaps and congratulations surrounded Sam.

"Awesome, man," Dennis yelped, grinning from ear to ear. "You *flew* over that guy!"

North had to punt and Alden took over. But Sam wasn't off the field for long. Tim Lopatt fumbled the ball after a short gain and North recovered. The defense held again. This time North tried a pass on third down, but it was poorly thrown.

Alden failed to make a first down. Tim made a nice six-yard gain, but Barry's third-down QB sneak came up short. Quickly, the game was settling into a defensive battle. They traded possessions again. North got a first down on an eight-yard pass, but then lost the ball on a fumble.

Alden took over and went to the air on first down. Nick caught Barry's pass and nearly broke free before being dragged down for a sixteen-yard gain. The Alden bench erupted with cheers, but Sam's heart sank. As much as he wanted the team to win, Barry's success continued to grate on him. He gave a cheer, pretending to be happy. At least it was great for Nick.

When Alden still couldn't score, Jack went in to punt. He sent the ball all the way to North's goal line, where a small North player caught it and headed up the left sideline. The first few players to take a shot at him missed. He cut back inside, and suddenly the Alden bench knew it was trouble. One fake and he was by Jack. Nick was giving chase, but the kid had a set of wheels. Nobody was catching him from behind. North converted the extra point and took the lead 7–0. The first half ended without another score.

After unsuccessful passes early in the second half, both coaches went to the running game. Sam was having a great game. He was sealing off the run on his side without a problem, and he nearly had one pass picked off, but it was just out of his reach. He didn't mind watching Barry's efforts sputter, either.

Late in the third quarter, Bob broke free around right end. He carried the ball twenty-six yards down to the North ten-yard line. From there, Barry took the option four yards and then Tim punched across for the score. Jack squibbed the extra point, so Alden still trailed 7–6. But now they had momentum.

North struck back with a complete pass for a first down, but Alden was still controlling the line. North runners were finding nowhere to go. Sam batted down the third-down pass, forcing North to punt.

Sam was halfway back. Jimmy Carlisle, the Alden safety, was the punt returner, but the North punter hit the ball badly. It floated lazily, coming right to Sam. He was surprised but he caught it and took off. He headed left until he saw a crowd of North uniforms and cut back. The first tackler to get at Sam took him high. How many times had Coach Kramden told his team—tackle the legs! Sam spun away easily. Another cut and he was in the open field, though hotly pursued. It was like a fantasy to Sam. He could almost hear the announcer as he ran: "McCaskill is breaking it open on the right sideline. He's at the thirty, the twenty!" But the North pursuit angled in on him. Sam was finally cut down from the side.

He got up to the shouts and leaps of his teammates. They slapped his helmet and shoulder pads. Sam smiled. Boy, did that ball feel good! As he left the field, the Alden offense came on. He looked up to see Barry crossing his path.

"Go get 'em," Sam said.

Barry looked surprised. "Yeah. Yeah, nice play, McCaskill."

Three plays later, Tim again pushed the ball across the goal line, this time carrying two tacklers with him. Alden took the lead for good. Jack knocked home the kick to make it 13–7, and when the game ended, Alden was undefeated.

9

The quick charge of victory only increased Sam's desire to play quarterback. He had been outstanding at cornerback in yesterday's game, but still thought he could quarterback better than Barry. Yet he had already had two full weeks of practice to show Coach Kramden his stuff. Did he deserve a second chance?

There was no practice Saturday. Sam's only plan was to go for an overdue haircut.

While a lot of kids were going to get their hair styled at the "Hair Shed" or "The Cuttery" at the

Cranbrook Mall, Sam went to Bill's Barbershop. The haircut was always good, and the barber also happened to be his father's older brother—and his favorite uncle.

It was just ten o'clock when Sam locked his tenspeed to the rack outside the barbershop. Sam was the first customer and he could see Uncle Bill taking a snooze in one of the chairs. Sam pushed through the door, which jingled a bell.

"Oh, hi, Sam. Just restin' my eyes," Uncle Bill said. "Your dad said you won yesterday. Congratulations."

"Thanks, Uncle Bill," said Sam, sitting down. He told his uncle all about the game and all the practices, the missed plays, the time he misunderstood Coach's instruction, and he told him that he still wanted to be quarterback.

"I don't know," Sam said. "I guess I should be happy. At least I'm a starter, and I did my best. But . . ."

"Sounds like the game didn't cure your quarterback fever."

"I guess not."

"Well, Sam, if you really want to play quarterback, you can't give up so easily."

When Charlie and Dennis had said the same thing,

it seemed impossible. But when it came from Uncle Bill, Sam believed it.

"But what can I do? I had my chance and I blew it. Why do I deserve a second chance?"

Uncle Bill mulled it over.

"Seems like the first step is talking to your coach."

"Me?"

"I'm certainly not going to do it for you."

"Talk to him?" Sam was disappointed. He had wanted to hear an easy answer. Going up to Coach Kramden and asking for another chance, well, it just seemed wrong, like begging. Anyway, he didn't want to talk to Coach.

"I don't think so," Sam said. "Just go and ask him, 'Please Mr. Coach, I really, really want to be quarterback. Pretty please.' That won't do any good."

"What do you expect me to tell you? That if you tap your heels together three times and say, 'There's no position like quarterback,' you'll be the starter?"

Sam laughed.

"But what if I ask and he says no?"

"Are you any worse off?"

"What if I get another chance and mess up?"

"I repeat, are you any worse off? Have you talked to your coach much?"

"Not really."

"Never asked him what your weak points are, or how to improve, or anything? Ever ask a question?"

Sam shook his head. "I guess I just don't like talking to grown-ups."

"What am I? The world's baldest six-year-old?"

"You're not a grown-up."

"Don't tell my wife that."

"I mean, you're just different. It's easy to talk to you. But with coaches and teachers . . . I don't know what to say. I sound stupid."

"C'mon, Sam. You're not so shy. How many times have I heard you bossing your friends around?"

Sam didn't like what he was hearing. Uncle Bill wasn't being any help at all. Sam changed the subject.

"Did you ever play football, Uncle Bill?"

"I played exactly one season when I was about fourteen or fifteen years old."

"What position did you play?"

"Left out," Uncle Bill said with a laugh.

"Really?"

"Yup. I was too slow for the backfield and too small for the line and too nice to be a linebacker."

"You didn't play at all?"

"I got in two games all year, one for about two minutes at defensive end. The other game was my big day. We were ahead by thirty or forty points. It was the last game of the season, I think. Coach was putting all the substitutes in as the game was winding down. With five minutes left, he says to me, 'Go in for Mulligan,' and I grab my helmet and run on the field. I tell Mulligan I'm coming in for him and ask him what position he's playing. 'Middle linebacker,' he says. Fine. Only one problem: Middle linebacker calls the defensive plays. Now, I'd given up hope of ever getting into a game, so I had totally forgotten the playbook. The team gets into the huddle and everyone is looking at me. I look around, take a peak at the offense like I'm trying to decide. All the time I'm stalling. I can't think of a single defensive play. Finally I say: 'Same thing as last time.' For the last five minutes of the game, ten straight plays, I called 'same thing as last time.' "

Sam was laughing. "Didn't anyone say anything?"

"They were all substitutes, too. They probably figured it was standard practice. Naturally, the other team scored a touchdown. And that was my greatest day in football."

Another customer came in and since Sam wanted to watch some games on TV that afternoon, he said good-bye. He went outside and started to unlock his bike. Then he remembered why he had come to see his uncle and went back into the shop.

"Forget something?" his uncle asked, clipping his customer's hair.

"Yeah," Sam said. "I'm supposed to get a haircut."

10

The week after the first game, practice was intense. The players had tasted action and they wanted more. They realized that everything Coach Kramden had been teaching them could lead to another win. They had seen for themselves how important it was to fire out of the three-point stance and how tackling with your arms was no good, that you needed to put your whole body to use. Now they were eager to learn more.

Although Sam joined in the growing excitement,

he still had quarterbacking on his mind. He kept thinking of Uncle Bill's advice. It seemed so simple. But the more Sam thought about it, the more he worried. Whenever he saw an opportunity to talk to Coach Kramden, his stomach churned with nervousness. And every time he put off approaching him, he felt even worse. *What if I do ask, and what if I do get another chance, and then mess up again? I'd look like a jerk!* The thought of failing a second time tied him up in knots.

Friday came and with it Alden's second game. Sam still hadn't spoken to Coach. He had just about given up.

Williamsport was supposed to be a good team but they had lost their first game to Bradley. The Alden players, coming off the win, were confident. The game was to be played at Williamsport, a 40-minute bus ride away.

Sam and Justin sat together, with Nick and Dennis in front of them. The bus was loud with excited chatter. Since his conversation with Dennis, Sam hadn't talked about playing quarterback. He didn't want his friends to think he was whining. But today Justin brought up the topic.

"Don't you think you should be quarterback?" he asked bluntly.

"I don't know." Sam shrugged.

"C'mon."

"He does," Dennis said. "Isn't that so?"

"Well, sure," Sam admitted. "I mean I wish I was good enough."

"You are, though," Dennis said. "You're better than Barry and tons better than Jack."

"Not according to Coach."

"Well, you didn't play your best before," Justin pointed out.

"Maybe Coach will let you try again," Nick said.

"At least you get to play, Sam. I got in for all of five minutes last week," Justin complained. "So much for Coach promising everyone would play at least a quarter."

"You're not quitting?" Dennis asked.

"No, I just don't know if football is my game, that's all. As soon as I can play on the soccer team, I'll do that instead."

"When does soccer start?"

"Ninth grade, I think," Justin answered.

"Maybe I'll play soccer, too," Sam said.

"No way," Dennis put in. "Football has been your favorite sport since second grade."

"Playing quarterback *was* my favorite sport," Sam said.

"You've got to try again," Dennis urged.

"I've got an idea," Nick said. "Let's kidnap Barry and Jack next Friday and leave them tied up in the old tree fort. Once Coach sees Sam play, he'll be the starter for sure."

"Great suggestion, Nick," Dennis said. "Seriously, Sam, you should ask Coach."

"It couldn't hurt," Justin agreed.

Sam still wasn't sure, but he appreciated their confidence. The four talked for the whole trip.

The Alden Panthers were rowdy and loud all through warm-ups. Once the game began, however, Williamsport quickly quieted them. The Williamsport kick returner took the opening kick seventy yards for a touchdown. The extra point was good and with only 22 seconds off the clock, Alden trailed by seven points.

The Alden offense took the field but made no headway. Two runs went nowhere, and on the third-down pass play, Barry was sacked. Jack at least managed to get off a good punt. Then Williamsport took over.

Sam finally got to take the field. He quickly discovered why his team was having such trouble. The end on his side was big. Sam could hardly believe this was a seventh-grader. He wondered why this guy wasn't playing fullback—until he noticed that their fullback was even bigger. The first play came to his side, an off-tackle run. Sam was ready for it, but he wasn't ready for the crushing block laid on him by the end. The runner was gone before Sam knew what hit him. Luckily, Dennis caught up and made the tackle after a seven-yard gain.

"They've got the horses," Sam said to Dennis as they gathered in the huddle.

"No joke," Dennis said. "They're huge."

The huddle came together.

"We've got to have gang tackles every time. They're big, so let's be quick," Dennis said, then he called the play. "43-Spread."

Firing off the line and pushing Alden back on every play, Williamsport crossed midfield and then made a first down. An attempted pass was off the mark. On third down, Sam fought off a block and made a key tackle on an end-around play. The Alden defense had held.

The two teams went back and forth. Williamsport intercepted one of Barry's passes but it was called back on a penalty. The Panthers, no longer so intimidated, were playing good defense, but the offense was going nowhere. Williamsport took over at Alden's fifteen-yard line, and with two runs brought it to the one. The quarterback sneak-punched into the end zone, and again the kick was good.

The ball was Alden's only briefly. Barry fumbled it away and the tired defense took the field. After an inside run for short yardage, they went to the pass. Sam backed into his coverage. He was man-to-man with the end, but already a step behind him when the pass came toward them. Sam leapt but the ball was just beyond his reach. The receiver caught it easily. He was gone and Williamsport now led by three touchdowns. Sam cursed himself.

Barry had been struggling, but Sam was surprised when Coach replaced him with Jack. The substitution didn't turn things around. Jack made a long run, but the offense again stalled. No one scored and the half ended with Alden losing, 21–0.

The players were hanging their heads at halftime. Coach tried to pep them up, but it was hard to be convincing.

"I know you guys think they're just too big, but you're wrong if you think we can't play with them," Coach said. "If we tighten up, we can get right back into the game. Execution. Discipline. Every man doing his job. Special teams: You guys have to stay in your lanes! We can't afford kick returns like that first one. All right, stay loose, stretch out. Drink a little water."

Alden took the ball first in the second half. They made a hard-fought first down on three short runs. They tried to pass—a 64-Blue, the post pattern— but Jack couldn't put any mustard on the ball. Williamsport intercepted and took over.

Then Alden got their first break. On third down, the quarterback floated a pass across the middle. The Williamsport receiver was there, but so was Dennis. He intercepted the ball easily and ran twenty yards before being knocked out of bounds. The Alden bench came to life, but not for long. The swarming Williamsport defense clogged up the Alden running game again. At least they were close enough so that Jack could try a fourth-down field goal. He made it, putting Alden on the board at last.

It was the first and last score for Alden that afternoon. Though the defense continued to play well, the offense was overmatched. Barry came back in, but he couldn't complete a pass. As Sam watched from the sideline, his frustration mounted, and the old wish came back stronger than ever. *Gimme one shot, just one chance,* he thought. *I can throw that ball.*

Sam watched Barry scramble away from a heavy

pass rush that forced him to dump the ball out of bounds. Sam turned and caught Dennis's eye. Both their faces showed the frustration of losing.

"We need you in there," Dennis said under his breath.

Sam didn't know what to say. He wished he deserved his friend's faith in him.

Williamsport recovered a fumble near the goal line and scored again. Barry completed a short pass— only the second completed pass for Alden all day.

The final score was Williamsport 28, Alden 3. The bus ride home was quiet.

11

The loss to Williamsport made Sam itch to get his hands on the ball. That weekend, Jill, Charlie, and Mr. McCaskill all took turns catching pass after pass. Dennis came by and they talked and threw it around for a while, too. When his dad asked what all the football was for, Sam said: "Just in case, that's all."

He finally decided to ask Coach Kramden for another try on Monday. Uncle Bill was right, it couldn't hurt. Still, Sam felt like he needed some moral support, so he bicycled down to the barbershop to get more advice.

"Another haircut already?" Uncle Bill asked. "Wait, let me guess. All the guys on the team are getting Mohawks?"

"Fat chance! I just stopped in to say hello."

His uncle finished cutting a customer's hair and sat down. Sam told him about the game and about his new determination to speak to Coach.

"Good for you," Uncle Bill said with a smile. "Just step right up to him and tell him what you think."

"I will, but it won't be easy."

"Nothing worth having comes easily. But don't be pushy, Sam. If the coach says no, you have to take him at his word."

"Okay, Uncle Bill, thanks. I'm going to do it. I'll let you know what Coach Kramden says."

"Kramden? Wait a second, not Paul Kramden?"

"Paul? No, I think it's Jerry, yeah, Jerry Kramden."

"Jerry Kramden! I remember little Jerry the pipsqueak." Uncle Bill laughed. "He was my friend Paul's little brother."

Sam could hardly believe his ears. Someone calling Coach "Jerry the pipsqueak"?

"Tell him I said hello," said Uncle Bill. "Or maybe

you better not. The last time I saw him was when Paul and I hung him in the coatroom by his underwear so he would quit following us around. He must have been eight, nine years old."

Sam was still laughing at the thought of his coach hanging by his underwear as he got on his bike. He started across the way when he suddenly spotted Coach Kramden! Coach was getting out of his car in front of the grocery store. Taken by surprise, Sam looked away quickly, pretended not to see him, and rode past. Then he glanced back to see Coach go into the grocery store.

Sam pulled his bike around, stopped, and stood up. He looked at the grocery store, flat and wide, its windows plastered with weekly specials. *I have to go in,* he thought. *It's now or never.*

Sam changed his mind three times before he finally stepped on the automatic doormat and into the store. He took a hand basket and began wandering up and down the aisles. As soon as he spotted Coach, Sam stepped back, took a deep breath, and walked forward, pretending to scan the shelves.

"Oh, hi, Coach."

"Hello, Sam, doing a little shopping?" He nodded to Sam's empty basket.

"Yeah, I, uh, just got started." The conversation

paused for a long few seconds and Sam's old fears took over.

"Nice to see you," he muttered and quickly turned away.

"Take it easy, Sam."

Coach reached for a loaf of bread.

Sam headed straight for the door. He was almost out when he stopped and turned around. He went down another aisle, picking things off the shelves, trying to build up his courage again. Finally, he saw Coach by the meat section.

Forget it, he thought, as another wave of anxiety took over. *I can't do it. That's all there is to it.*

Then he looked at Coach Kramden again and suddenly imagined "Jerry the pipsqueak" hanging in the coatroom, hollering. Sam made his way down the aisle.

"Coach?"

"Yes, Sam?"

Sam hesitated.

"Got some stuff now, huh?" Coach said, looking at Sam's basket. Sam looked down. He had marshmallows, licorice, pickled herring, and three packs of batteries. He started to blush, but instead he plunged ahead.

"I've been wanting to talk to you," he began. "It's

about, well, it's about being quarterback. I want another shot. I know I had a fair chance. And I don't mean to be asking for special treatment or favors or anything. But I've just got to have another shot. I can play the position, I know I can, and I . . ."

"Slow down, Sam," Coach interrupted.

Sam caught his breath.

"Well, that's all, really."

Coach nodded thoughtfully, leaning on his cart.

"You know I've always appreciated your dedication," Coach began.

Sam got a bad feeling.

"But I've got to be fair to Barry and Jack."

"I know."

Coach mulled it over. Finally, he spoke, nodding.

"Okay. Take another shot. I'll give you practice time and we'll see how it goes. I can see that it really matters to you."

A wide smile spread across Sam's face.

"You won't regret this, Coach," he said excitedly. "I'll see you Monday."

Sam rushed off, hurriedly putting the items from his basket back on the shelves. Another shopper was going to find a jar of pickled herring among the marshmallows.

Once outside, Sam ran to Uncle Bill's and told him what had just happened.

"Thanks for pushing me, Uncle Bill!"

"I knew you could do it," his uncle said.

Sam was bursting with energy. He rode his bike home at top speed. But even as he flew along he knew this was just a small first step. This wasn't just his second chance—it was his last chance.

12

"McCaskill in at quarterback."

Sam had been waiting all practice to hear those words. They sounded great.

Earlier, Coach had come by Sam's locker to offer a brief refresher course on quarterbacking. Sam had started to say he didn't need one, but he thought again. That was the same mistake he'd made before: not listening, not talking, not asking questions.

"Sure. That would really help."

"All right," Coach said, sitting down. "You know the offense. We're running most of the time. For every play, one of the split ends will run in with the play. If you have a problem out there, don't be afraid to call time-out. That's better than blowing a play."

Coach went on to talk him through the basics, to explain what his responsibilities were, and which details to concentrate on. Sam had heard it before, but hearing it again helped him focus on the game.

Sam now took his place in the offensive huddle. After the scrimmage lineups were set, Alan ran in with the play: 24-Red. A simple handoff to Tim.

"Seventy-two! Nineteen! Hut! Hut!"

The snap came but Sam didn't get it right. It hit his thumb and squirted back. All he could do was jump on the ball. Coach whistled the play dead.

The excitement was gone. Instead, a feeling of calm determination came over Sam. He wasn't angry at himself. He knew he wasn't going to drop the ball again. At last, everything was going to be all right. Playing for the team was going to be like playing in the backyard, no worries, just fun.

For a change, Sam was the underdog, fighting his way up from the bottom. Before, he had expected to be on top; now he knew he had to *make* his own success.

The next play was the option. Sam held the ball until the last possible minute, drawing the tacklers to him. He faked into them and flipped the ball neatly back to Bob, who galloped down the sideline for a long gain.

Sam ran a dozen plays and threw five passes. All but one were caught and the incomplete pass came only because the receiver looked away too soon. Sam also broke a QB sneak for a ten-yard run. Then Coach Kramden gave him one last play: a pass, 64-Blue. Nick was the primary receiver. In the huddle, Sam called the play, and as they broke, grabbed Nick's jersey.

"Take it extra long, Nick."

"You got it."

There was no contest. Nick put a single fake on the cornerback and took off. Sam cranked the ball. It was a beauty, spinning like a top, twenty-five yards in the air, right into Nick's chest. The corner didn't even chase him.

That was Monday. The next day's practice wasn't as perfect, but on Wednesday, Sam noticed Jack Sylvester in his huddle. He knew then he had done something right. Jack was in to practice at tight end. On Thursday, Coach made it official when he read the next game's starters. Barry was still starting, but Sam was his backup. Never had Sam imagined that playing backup could feel so good.

South Colby was another away game. On the bus Nick, Justin, Dennis, and Sam sat together again. Bored with his part-time role at split end, Justin had started keeping statistics on the team.

"During practice this week you completed over sixty percent of your passes," he told Sam. "That's better than Fran Tarkenton's lifetime average."

"Gee, I guess I should skip right to the NFL."

"Bob and Tim ran for about the same total yardage in the four practices, but Bob averaged more yards per carry—over five yards."

"Yeah," Dennis said, "except he knew exactly what the defense was going to do. He's been playing against them every day for four weeks."

"I thought of that," Justin said. "And it's true, but the defense pretty much knew what the offensive plays were. So both sides had about the same advantage."

"Okay, so what does your pocket calculator say about our chances against South Colby?" Nick asked.

"Well . . ." Justin raised his eyebrows.

"What?"

"Not so good," he admitted. "South shut out North

last week, twenty-eight to nothing, and we only beat them by six points, so . . ." He shrugged.

"Doesn't mean a thing," Sam said. "We're going to win."

Somehow Sam's confidence seemed more convincing than all of Justin's figuring.

"Did you win? Did you win?"

When Sam got home that night, Charlie was waiting for him out in the driveway. He was throwing a tennis ball onto the roof and catching it when it came down. Charlie grabbed Sam to tackle him, but his older brother dodged and ran onto the lawn. Charlie followed him to try again, but Sam wrestled him down.

"Did you win?" Charlie repeated.

"Maybe."

"You're smiling, you must have won."

"I'm not smiling," Sam said, trying to put on a serious face, but then smiling again. "You know why I'm happy? I played a little quarterback and I did pretty well, too."

"But did you win?"

"Maybe."

"Tell me the whole game," Charlie said.

"Well, we started out slowly. I played cornerback

in the first half. Jimmy Carlisle made a great interception to stop South Colby's first long drive."

"Why didn't you make the interception?"

"Because I was nowhere near it, dimwit. Do you want to hear about the game or not?"

"I'll be quiet."

"Okay, they scored first after making an interception off Barry. That was in the first quarter. In the second quarter Nick ran an end-around play for over twenty yards to get us close. Then Bob scored the touchdown on another good run. Jack missed the extra point, though, so we were still behind, 7–6."

"Get to the part where you play."

"Okay, okay. South scored a field goal and a touchdown in the second quarter. The touchdown was on a punt return. It was really bad. Four of our players should have tackled him."

"Why didn't you tackle him?"

"Because I was on the sideline watching."

"Oh, yeah."

"At half-time . . ."

"Was there a marching band at halftime?"

"No. Now, at halftime Coach told me I would be in at quarterback to start the third quarter. I was psyched. The first possession was bad. We made three short runs and then punted, but they did the same thing and we took over again. This time Coach called a pass on first down and Jack—he was playing tight end—made a great catch for a first. A few runs later Tim busted up the middle for another long gain. We came down the field like a machine. Then South held us near the goal. It was third down. I scrambled to the right side and made a great pass to Nick for the touchdown. Jack made the kick and we were close again. It was, let's see, seventeen to thirteen."

"You won, right?"

"You want me to spoil the ending?"

"No."

"Okay, anyway, we had another good drive, but they held us scoreless the rest of the third quarter. After that Barry came back at quarterback."

"Why did the coach take you out?"

"Because Barry has played more, I guess."

"But you played better."

Sam just shrugged. He thought so, too.

"So what else happened?" Charlie asked, still impatient.

"South scored one more time on a long run, and that was all. Twenty-four to thirteen."

"You lost?" Charlie asked with surprise.

"Yup."

"What a crummy ending."

"Sorry, next time I'll tell you *The Three Bears*."

"When are Mom and Dad going to take me to see one of your games?"

"Maybe next Friday. We're playing Lincoln at night. And the week after that we play on a Saturday."

"Is that your last game?"

"Yep."

"Is it against a good team?"

"The best. Bradley."

13

Abraham Lincoln was the other junior high school in Cranbrook. Both Lincoln and Alden were 1–2. The upcoming game would not only put one team ahead in the standings, but would also determine which of Cranbrook's rival junior highs would claim the town's bragging rights.

The pep club put up banners in the Alden cafeteria. For the first time, students were finding out who was on the football team. All the attention didn't make much difference to the Alden Panthers though. They were too worried about losing the game.

Last week's loss had been hard on the team. South hadn't been that much better than they were —they weren't big, like Williamsport—but they had still won the game pretty easily. It was discouraging.

Sam, Nick, and Dennis were eating lunch in the cafeteria.

"Quite a fuss, huh?" Sam asked, pointing to one of the banners.

"Oh, yeah, we're really school heroes," Nick said. "My arm is sore from signing autographs."

"Hey, at least it's something," Sam said. "I don't understand why everyone on the team is acting like we've already lost to Lincoln. It's ridiculous. They've lost as many games as we have."

"Nobody is planning to lose," Dennis put in. "It just seems silly to pretend this is such a big game."

"Every game is a big game," Sam declared. "If we win today, and Williamsport beats Bradley, and then we beat Bradley next week, our record will be three and two. We'd tie for the conference title."

"Beat Bradley? Get real," Nick said. "Bradley crushed both North and Lincoln."

"Nothing's impossible."

"Well, anyway, it's going to be great playing under the lights tonight," Nick said. "Really cool."

They all nodded. Most of their games were played in the afternoons. The Lincoln–Alden game would be played at night on the Cranbrook High School field, because there was always a larger turnout— if you can call 100 people large—for games between the town's rival teams.

Justin arrived at the table with his lunch tray and they scooted around to give him room.

"Here's the Panthers' newest superstar," Dennis said.

"The lean, mean fighting machine, Justin 'White Shoes' Johnson," Nick chimed in.

"What can I say? Coach finally recognized my incredible talent," Justin said. Yesterday, he had been named to the starting team for the first time, at safety.

"Actually," he continued, "I think Coach is just trying to give everyone a chance."

"No way," Dennis said. "You earned that spot. And you should be getting in at end, too."

Just then, the masking tape gave out on one end of a large banner reading GO PANTHERS. The long piece of brown paper with blue paint fluttered noisily from above the food line to the ground. The guys rolled their eyes and laughed.

That evening, the players gathered at Alden to suit up for the game. When they were ready they took a short bus ride to Cranbrook High. Excitement was beginning to mount.

Despite Sam's standout performance last week, Coach still had Barry slotted as the starting quarterback. Sam didn't mind so long as he got into the game.

The glare of the lights on the field was every bit as terrific as Sam had imagined. He felt almost like they were on TV. His little brother's arrival at his side reminded him that this wasn't exactly the Rose Bowl.

"Hey, Sam!"

"Hi, Charlie."

"We got seats right in the front row," Charlie said, pointing back to where Sam could see his whole family. They waved and Sam waved back.

"Doesn't look like it was too hard to get good seats," Sam said. There were about fifty people scattered throughout the bleachers that could hold 2,000. "You're not really supposed to be out here on the sideline, Charlie."

"All right, all right, I'm going. Good luck."

But the only luck the Alden Panthers had was bad. As usual, their special teams messed up. Early in the first quarter a Lincoln punt took a wicked bounce and hit the Alden return man who was trying to get out of the way. As soon as it touched him, it was a live ball, and Lincoln recovered it just 17 yards out of the end zone. Lincoln's main offensive weapon was their big fullback, Gorman Paderowski. He wasn't fast. In fact, he was pretty darn slow, and over-weight, too, but he didn't go down easily. Relying on Paderowski on almost every play, Lincoln ran the ball straight ahead, made a first down, and then pushed it in for the first TD. For the fourth straight game, Alden had given up the first points.

Sam was angry at himself. Playing cornerback, he had let himself be taken out of the play on one of Paderowski's runs to his side. He watched Barry lead the Alden offense onto the field. They got nothing on two runs and then Barry threw away an easy chance for a complete pass. The game bogged down quickly. A number of penalties were called on both teams. Barry brought Alden close enough for two field-goal chances, but Jack only made one of them. In the meantime, Lincoln added a touchdown and a field goal.

As the end of first half neared, Lincoln led 17–3. They had the ball deep in their own end. The play was one Alden had already seen a half-dozen times, a simple handoff to Paderowski. But now Alden was worn out. Paderowski knocked aside the line and then slipped out of Dennis's grasp. He was building up momentum. Only one Alden player stood between him and the open field: Justin Johnson, all 86 pounds of him. Sam was getting up to give chase as he watched the confrontation. Paderowski didn't bother to fake, he just rolled ahead like a tank. Sam could hardly bear to watch. He almost wished Justin would get out of the way.

The two players collided. Paderowski slowed for a moment, then kept going, even with Justin clinging to one of his legs. Sam was up now and ran after them. Paderowski continued to carry Justin until Sam and some others caught up and pulled them down.

"Nice tackle, Justin," Sam said, helping him up.

"Once. Just once and never again," Justin said. "If you guys let him through one more time I'm just going to wave at him when he goes by."

Sam and the others laughed.

The half ended without another score.

Coach gave Sam the nod. It was his turn to take

the helm, but turning things around wasn't going to be easy. Lincoln drove the length of the field to score again, pushing their lead to 24–3.

When Sam looked around the huddle on his first play, he saw grim, tired expressions. He saw broken spirits. He saw a team that had given up. His own spirits were sinking, but he rallied against them. He wasn't going to go down without a fight. He realized it was his turn to give a pep talk.

"You guys look like a bunch of quitters," Sam barked. The players suddenly came to attention. They looked at each other. Sam was a little surprised at himself, too. "Now, c'mon, let's play some ball. 28-Blue on three. 28-Blue on three."

No quarterback had ever spoken like that in the huddle. Not Barry. Not Jack. Sam heard some grumbling. He could tell that some of the guys weren't too sure they liked this new attitude. Being QB didn't mean that Sam could push them around. But at the same time, they realized that what Sam was saying was true, they had been giving up.

Despite the murmurs, Sam's little speech sparked the team. At the snap, the line fired out with renewed drive. Bob took the handoff and found daylight. The linebacker grabbed him after five yards, but Bob pressed forward for three more yards before he went down. Three teammates were there to help him up.

Alden was back on track. Sam led them down the field. He contributed a key third-down pass completion and a ten-yard run on the option play. Bob took off on a 17-yard romp. Finally, Tim carried three tacklers into the end zone for the score. Alden had hit pay dirt. Jack kicked the extra point.

The score was 24–10, but more importantly, the whole Alden team was brought back into the game. The defense swarmed over Lincoln, bringing down Paderowski with gang tackles. The offense ground out yardage, but stalled before they could score again. Twice, they were hurt by penalties. The game became a standoff played in the middle of the field, with neither team able to put together a sustained drive.

Ten minutes were left in the game. It was beginning to look desperate for the Panthers. They took possession at the 38-yard line. As Sam jogged toward the huddle, he glanced down the length of the field. The end zone looked a long way off.

Tim carried the ball five yards on the first play, but an end-around play backfired for a loss on the next play. Alden was left with a third down, eight yards to go. Nick ran in with the play: 60-Blue, the down-and-out pattern with Nick as primary receiver.

Sam was ready to pass, but they had run the play too many times already. He was afraid Lincoln would see it coming. He called the play once, then he addressed Nick.

"Run the pattern, but I'm not gonna throw it right away. Cut back in. Got it?"

"Got it."

"I'm gonna need extra time back there," Sam said to the linemen. "Give it to me."

They took their places. For a moment Sam was aware of the cool night air, blowing at his back, and the glare of the lights flickering overhead. He made the call, the snap came, and he backpedaled. The rush came strong. Sam had to turn and go deeper to buy time. Nick cut out, then back. He was open, but way down the field. Sam set and fired. Immediately he was knocked to the ground and buried. He couldn't see a thing. All he had to go by were the cheers. But who were they for? By the time he stood up, Nick was in the end zone, ball held aloft.

Coach Kramden called for the two-point conversion. If they could score the two points now, they would be within one touchdown of tying the score. The ball was placed at the three-yard line. Coach called for the QB option play.

Sam took the snap and ran. The Lincoln defenders

were on him too quickly. He flipped the ball back to Bob, but he, too, was surrounded. Bob fell short and the score remained 24–16. The clock now showed three minutes to play.

Alden tried an onside kick, but Lincoln recovered. Time was ticking off the clock with every play. Alden's only hope was to force Lincoln to punt after three plays. If they could score another touchdown fast enough *and* make the two-point conversion, Alden could tie.

The first play gained just two yards, but as Paderowski broke through the defense on the second, Alden's faint hopes faded. Paderowski was tackled, but only after making the first down. The game was out of reach. Lincoln ran three more plays and it was over.

14

Starting quarterback.

Sam finally had the job that had filled his day-dreams and nightmares for weeks. He had come back. He had taken his last chance and made good.

Unfortunately, the team he was quarterbacking was in sad shape.

Alden had run their record to an unimpressive one win and three losses. Their near comeback against Lincoln had boosted their confidence for a while. They had given it their best shot. After all, it wasn't whether you won or lost but how you played the game, right?

Wrong. On Monday their classmates let them know that close only counts in horseshoes and darts. They had lost to Lincoln. Period.

"Hey, Sam," Dave Zinsser called out from across the cafeteria. He was in Sam's English class. "When's the next game for the Alden *Pussycats*?"

All day it was more of the same. "Lincoln mauled you guys," "I'm transferring to Lincoln"—every wise guy in school had something to say, and not all of them were that polite. The gibes didn't seem very funny to the players.

When they gathered for Monday's practice, Sam could see that the team had no fire. They ran through their exercises without enthusiasm. It wasn't just the loss that was getting them down. Bradley, their opponent in the final game, was still undefeated, coming off a big win over Williamsport. Nobody in school thought they had a chance. Even Sam had his doubts. He was quarterback at last, but what good would that be if his team was already giving up? *At least things can't get any worse,* thought Sam.

Tuesday morning, Alden's slim chances got slimmer. Tim Lopatt, the big fullback, sprained his ankle in gym class. His football season was over.

Practice that afternoon was grim. No one was concentrating, and play was sloppy. Coach Kramden didn't lose his temper, but his patience seemed to be running out.

Wednesday afternoon, the players gathered again, but instead of running the usual starting drills, Coach sat everyone down.

"I've never pretended to be a big speech maker and I'm not going to start now," he began, "but I do have something to say. One thing, really, and that is that you *can* beat Bradley."

He let the words sink in. The players exchanged doubtful glances. Nobody was buying it. What about Tim's injury and the fact that Bradley had beaten three teams that had beaten them? Pep talks couldn't change the facts. Sam wanted to believe Coach more than anyone, but even he thought they didn't have a chance. Coach started to talk again.

"We caught some bad breaks this season, but we've played tough for the most part. I know that we're gonna miss Tim's running. I'm not blind. And I can see that none of you believe what I'm saying, but all I can do is say it again. I've got no secrets, no magic, but I do know something about football, and I know that if you want to, you can upset Bradley."

Practice started off just like the rest of the week:

sloppy plays, no second efforts, no talk. But Sam sensed that something had changed. Coach Kramden had planted an idea, a little voice that said: "Maybe, just maybe he's right."

Things started to change. When Sam took the QB option and turned it inside, he was met by two tacklers, but he spun out of their grip and plowed five more yards before a gang brought him down.

On the next play, Dennis charged in on a blitz, leapt, and batted away an attempted pass.

The Alden Panthers were back in the game. They were whooping it up. The offensive and defensive lines were banging heads. Sam's offense was clicking. It was crunch time, gut-check time, and Alden was pulling it together.

Over the next two days, Alden worked hard as a team. The change was for real. They knew that they were a long shot to beat Bradley, but they weren't going to throw in the towel.

On Saturday, Bradley came to town.

Game time was set for 11 A.M. The small set of bleachers by the Alden Junior High field wasn't even close to full, but the whole McCaskill family was there to watch Sam play. Uncle Bill was there, too.

The first half, however, didn't give them much to cheer about. Sam hardly ever had a chance to get set in the pocket before the rushers were all over him. The running game was no more successful. It was easy to see how Bradley had won all four of their games. They had some big players, especially on the line. There was never any confusion in their play, either. Every player seemed to know exactly where he was supposed to be. The defense swarmed over Alden.

Luckily, Bradley played conservatively on offense. They never threw the ball unless it was third-and-long, and since Alden knew that was a passing down, they kept Bradley from making a completion. On the other hand, the Bradley runners were tough. They only broke a couple of long runs, but they always seemed to get the three-yarder when they needed it. Their drives took a long time, but they worked. All that Alden could manage in response was one drive built on two medium pass completions and one terrific 34-yard run by Bob Donovan. They didn't get into the end zone, but Jack knocked home the field goal. They were lucky to go into halftime trailing 14–3.

Sam grabbed a handful of sliced oranges and found a place to sit down. On the other side of the field, he could see the Bradley coach flailing his arms as he gave his players an angry lecture. In contrast, Coach

Kramden just looked through his clipboard during most of halftime. Then, just as they were about to get set to start the second half, he called for everyone's attention.

"You've done a great job of controlling these guys. We've got to keep it up. Now, I'm going to do something a little different for the second half. Maybe we can throw Bradley for a loop."

The players looked at one another. They edged forward on the bench to play close attention. What was Coach Kramden thinking?

"We've stuck to the running game most of the time, just like everyone in this league, but I want to see if we can shake things up a little. Let's put the ball in the air and see if we can't turn this game around."

His words were music to Sam's ears. When Alden took the field, Coach sent in the play. Post-pattern long for Nick. On first down.

Sam repeated the play to the huddle. They set it up and Sam took the snap. He ran back quickly, but before Nick could even make his cut, Sam was sacked. He slapped his leg in frustration. If only he had scrambled out of the way. Alan Broadstreet relayed in from the sideline with the next play. Same thing. Sam looked at him disbelievingly. He glanced at the sideline where Coach was looking right at him.

Coach nodded yes and a grin spread across Sam's face.

This time the line managed to hold back the rush just long enough. Sam found his man and gave the ball a ride. It was just slightly overthrown but Nick dove and grabbed it. A nifty 18-yard combination and suddenly the Alden team came alive. Sam made two out of three more and suddenly they were closing in. The Bradley defense had never seen anything like this. All the teams in the league relied on running. Bradley tried to adjust, backing off the line quickly to look for the pass, but the next play was the QB-Option. Sam dished the ball to Bob, who broke outside almost all alone. He faked out one man and carried it in for the score. Jack missed the kick, leaving Bradley ahead 14-9.

Their passing offense had paid off right away, but Alden still had Bradley's offense to contend with. The long slow march began and nothing they did could stop it for long. Bradley scored again, making the kick, and led 21-9.

The game turned into a contrast of styles. Throughout the third quarter, Alden's passing continued to baffle the Bradley defenders, though they only scored once. Sam made nine out of fourteen attempts, giving up one interception. At the same time, Bradley's machinelike running game was devastatingly effective. Alden kept them out of the end zone—giving up one field goal—but couldn't keep their ball-control offense from eating up the clock. The third quarter ended with Bradley leading 24–16.

There were no doubts left on the Alden squad. They were still close, very close, and there were ten minutes on the clock. Coach Kramden was right. They could win.

Still going to the air, Sam led Alden on a long drive, but Bob fumbled the ball away. Bradley came rumbling back, but stalled at midfield, thanks to an offsides penalty. Again, they traded possessions without scoring. The clock was on Bradley's side.

Then Dennis intercepted one of the rare Bradley passes and returned it ten yards. A scoring pass from Sam to Alan was called back because of a holding penalty and they had to settle for a field goal.

The Panthers had gotten back to within a touchdown, 24–19, but now there were just three minutes left. And Bradley had the ball.

Sam watched on the sideline, nervously pacing. All he needed was one more shot, one more chance. On the third play, the Bradley runner rumbled end-around for a first down.

Bradley was still deep in its own territory, though. If the defense could force a punt now, Alden would be within range. On the next play, the Bradley half-back smashed up the middle and carried two tacklers all the way for another first. Alden's hopes were fading.

Then Paul Dominick shot into the backfield and tackled the Bradley runner for a loss. Two more runs went for short yardage. It was fourth down. Bradley would have to punt. Just 35 seconds were on the clock.

The punt was poor, but Alden couldn't return it and it took a Bradley bounce. As Sam led the offense onto the field, Alden was 57 yards away from victory. The first play was a 64-Blue, down and out to Alan.

Sam took the snap and in a flash saw that the blitz was on. All three linebackers rushed in. Immediately he dumped the ball to a startled Jack. Somehow Jack hung on to the ball and found himself with running room. He ran 23 yards down the sideline before the defense forced him out, stopping the clock.

Pay dirt was still a long way off, and with 14 seconds on the clock, Alden was down to their last play. Justin ran in from the sideline with the call: 66-Red. The fly pattern, with Nick the receiver.

Sam took the snap and backpedaled, pretending

to look left. The defensive end broke in on him. It was too soon to throw. Sam had to duck and scramble outside. Suddenly the pass blocking was a shambles. Nick was covered. Another tackler came at Sam, who whirled and retreated again. Now Nick was too far downfield. Out of the corner of his eye, Sam saw Justin coming back toward him, hands up and open. It was his only shot. He threw the ball.

The Bradley defender was close enough to make a play for it. He leaped and deflected the pass, but it bounced up off his hands and back into the air. The ball fell softly into Justin's hands. He turned and headed for the end zone. It was a footrace. The Bradley safety had the only chance, racing in at an angle as Justin sprinted for the goal line. They met at the two, but Justin dove and crossed into the end zone for the score. The Alden bench went wild. Jack went in and added the extra point, but they didn't need it. The score wouldn't change again. It was Alden 26, Bradley 24.

They had done it. Alden had won.

The guys all hooted and hollered and jumped on each other. Even Coach Kramden was grinning and slapping backs left and right. They lifted Justin— the unlikeliest hero—onto their shoulders. Amid the hoopla Sam smiled up at the bleachers. His parents gave him thumbs-up. Charlie and Jill were jumping up and down, and Uncle Bill held both arms high in victory.

"Who told you?" Dennis said, grabbing Sam happily around the neck. "Who told you that we had to have you at quarterback? Me, that's who!"

"What can I say?" Sam said. "You're a genius. You and my kid brother."

"I'll tell you something," Nick chipped in. "You know what this was? This was the first game of next season. Next year we're going to take this league to the cleaners. We're going to win it all."

When the celebration quieted down, the players headed to the locker room. Sam spent a few moments happily thinking about the triumph. The season was over. He had gotten a second chance and had proven that he deserved it. With the win, the Alden Panthers' record was final at two wins, three losses.

It wasn't a winning record, but for some reason, it sure felt like one.